WINGFIN AND TOPPLE

Wingfin

CLEVELAND AND NEW YORK

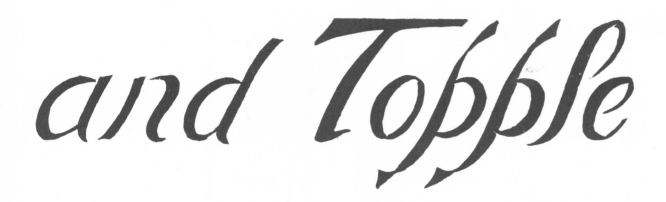

and Topple

by **EVANS G. VALENS, JR.**

pictures by **CLEMENT HURD**

THE WORLD PUBLISHING COMPANY

Published by The World Publishing Company

2231 West 110th Street, Cleveland 2, Ohio

Published simultaneously in Canada by

Nelson, Foster & Scott Ltd.

Library of Congress Catalog Card Number: 62-16362

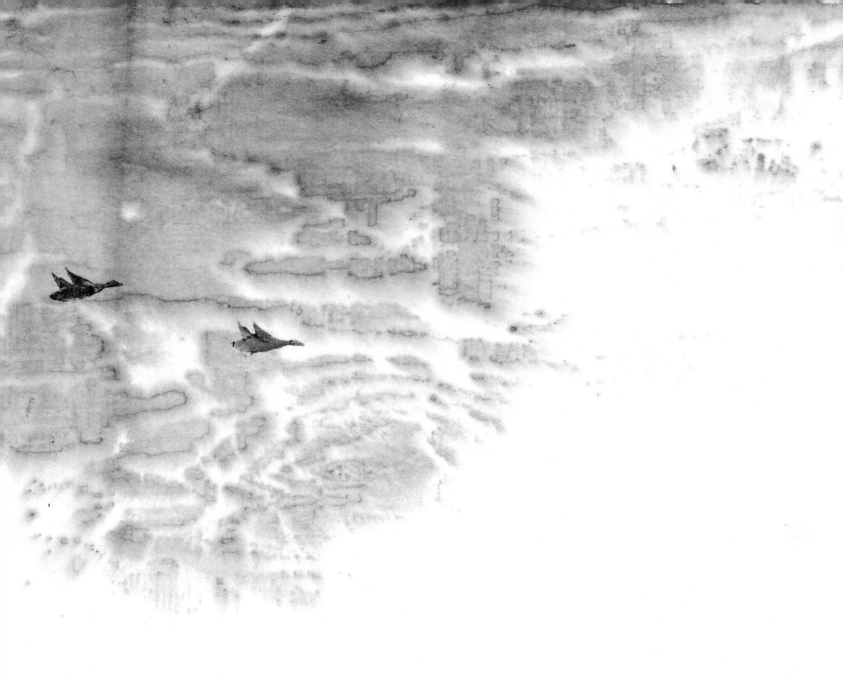

THE fat sun sat upon the ocean like a tangerine, bulging, orange-red. It quickly sank, drowning without a sound. The light on one last high cloud went out. The waves rolled over, whispered, sighed.

Far beneath the slumbering surface, in a sea-weed forest, darted restless, lean young fish. All were herring, sleek and trim, except for one: The herring called him Topple, for he stumbled on his fins.

"They made your fins too long," they said.

Indeed they were, twelve times as long as ordinary fins; when Topple spread them they caught hold like anchors, tripped him, rolled him belly up.

That night the herring headed for the open sea, but Topple cowered in the safety of the floating grasses he had always known.

Deserted, Topple hovered there between the bright green shimmer of the surface and the blackness of the ocean floor.

Then suddenly, deep in the sea-green shadows, a stranger with big yellow eyes appeared, a handsome fish with straight blue back and two great fins that folded close along his sides.

"Poor fish," said Topple. "You're just like me; they made your fins too long."

"Too *long?*" said Wingfin. "I am proud that I have wings for fins and fins for wings."

"What kind of fish would wish for wings?"

"A fish that loves the freedom of the air."

"The freedom of the *where?*"

"The air."

Topple rolled his yellow eyes. "Oh?" he said and dived below to find a crab he'd known. "Please tell me, What is air?"

"Stupid!" snapped the crab. "Air's what leaks from submarines."

"I'm not so sure," a sea horse said, clinging with its knobbly tail to sea vines in the floating jungle. "Air is silver bubbles on the sea leaf. Sometimes they fizzle up my back."

An octopus unknotted his arms, glanced over his shoulders, and burbled, "Why, air is what always goes up!" He hiccupped twice. Two bubbles rose through the water, round and white, rose to the top, and were suddenly gone with a *pop*.

Aha! So *there* is where air is!

"Of course," said Topple knowingly, "the freedom of the air. But how and why?"

"You fly," said Wingfin, swimming toward the rippled light above where sunshine played upon the ceiling of the sea.

"Lesson one: A fish, if he flies, does not fly high but low, as low as a skipping stone."

Then he was gone . . . a circle spreading where he'd been, a shadow wrinkling on the waves.

Topple followed, shot into the air . . . and fell. The water wrenched his outstretched fins.

"Lesson two: Whatever you do, remember to tuck in your fins when you're through."

Topple whipped his tail and swam again, faster . . . faster . . . till the water stung along his scales. Up through the roof of the sea he flung himself, flicked wide both fins. . . .

And suddenly the world was bright and cool and dry as he was lifted on the breeze. Swift and sure he soared, cool as a feather, scudding easily above the waves that flipped and snapped and spit below.

The sky above was fever-blue, punctured by the white hot circle of the sun. Its arching dome rested like a giant's cup turned upside down upon the great flat saucer of the sea.

Topple's lean tail ticked the wave tops. He folded up his fins, fanlike, and dropped back into the sea. The water felt as thick and slow as glue. Up, up again for a dip in the air . . . his spread-finned shadow flashed across the backs of herring feeding close beneath the surface of the sea.

"A magic fish," the herring said. And then when Topple splashed among them, "*He*'s the one who stayed at home because he stumbled on his fins!"

The herring threaded through the sea grass like the fingers of a comb while Topple soared and dipped and made the ocean foam. Far away along the saucer's edge, along the sea's horizon, the water was rumpled and no longer level but bumpy and lumpy and high. The ocean's in trouble, he thought. It's piled up in a hump.

"That's land," said the herring. "Beaches and rocks. If you fly there, you'll dry up and die."

Suddenly the sea was crowded, leaving scarcely room enough to wave a tail. "Quit shoving," said the herring, packed like seaweed in a sack.

"A net! A net! It's all around on every side. We'll all be caught and fried!"

Topple charged the net. He gnashed his teeth and lashed his tail. He slashed. He smashed. But he couldn't break out of the closing net, or under it, or through it.

Then he remembered: the freedom of the air.

Up he swam with thrashing tail and thrust his body toward the sky.

Fins wide, he glided from the trap, sailed freely over the crescent of floating corks that held the net, and dove into the safe green sea beyond.

Alone and breathless and afraid, Topple waved his weary tail and headed seaward toward the setting sun.

Black clouds gathered and the ocean's roof dimpled with the rain. The waves spoke darkly. Lightning slit the sky.

All night Topple swam. When morning came the surface was alive with sunlight sparkling like an oceanful of stars.

The glints of light grew larger and became a thousand leaping, splashing fish with bodies silver in the morning sun. With them was Wingfin.

"Lesson three: Don't fly alone; stay clear of nets; keep well away from beaches."

Topple swiftly joined the throng of soaring fish with fins too long. A bright wind whipped the spray from cresting whitecaps, scattering the clean smell of salt across the freshened air. The sea was gay with flashing fins like wind-blown tinsel in the sun.